BOBO'S MAGIC WISHES

First-Start® Legends

BOBO'S MAGIC WISHES
A STORY FROM PUERTO RICO

Retold by Janet Palazzo-Craig
Illustrated by Charles Reasoner

Troll

There once was a young man named Juan Bobo. It was his job to watch the king's sheep.

One night, the king's wheat field was
trampled. "Who did this?" cried the king.

The king ordered his men to take turns guarding the wheat. But night after night, the guards fell asleep and more of the wheat was ruined.

At last, it was Juan's turn to watch the field. Off he went, carrying his dinner and a rope.

Juan sat in the field and ate his dinner.
Bread and honey! What a sweet, sticky
dinner! Then Juan fell asleep.

But not for long! Soon the ants came for *their* dinner. They bit Juan again and again.

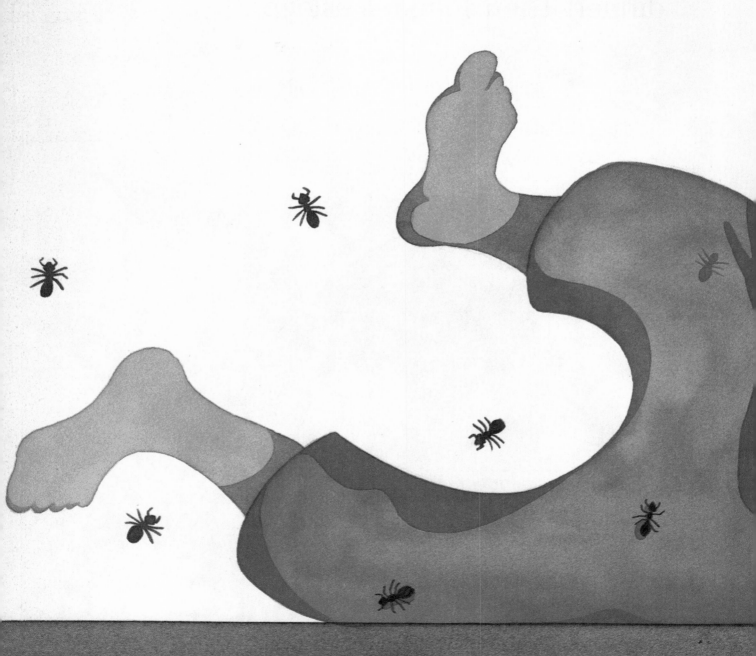

"Ow, ouch," cried Juan.

Finally, the ants left. But the ant bites were so itchy that Juan could no longer sleep.

Suddenly, Juan saw a beautiful horse running through the king's wheat. Its mane and tail were many different colors. Quickly, Juan used his rope to catch the horse.

The horse spoke. "If you let me go, I will give you seven hairs from my coat. Each hair will give you a wish."

Juan let the horse go. The seven hairs were his.

When Juan got home, he told his brothers about the horse. They laughed at him. They did not think he was too smart.

Then the brothers left. They were going to the castle. They had heard that the princess was very sad and there was a reward for anyone who could make her laugh.

Juan scratched the itchy ant bites. "I wish these bites would stop itching!" he cried.

Juan was suddenly covered in mud. The mud made the bites stop itching. The red hair was gone!

"Now I am hungry," said Juan. "I wish for a sausage that never gets smaller."

His wish was granted! This time the orange hair was gone.

"Now I will wish for new clothes," said Juan. "Then I will go help my brothers."

Juan was soon dressed in beautiful clothes. The yellow hair was gone.

"I am beautiful," said Juan. "Now I wish for a fine horse."

In front of him, there appeared a fine horse. The green hair was gone.

Juan got on the
horse. The horse
began to run!

The horse ran and ran. Juan could not hold on. Off he fell. His new clothes were ruined!

Buzz-buzz-buzz! Juan had fallen on a beehive! Angry bees buzzed. "I wish these bees would go away," cried Juan.

At once, birds filled the air. They chased the angry bees. Now the blue hair was gone.

"That horse was too fast," said Juan. "I wish for a donkey."

Suddenly, a donkey appeared. One more hair was gone. Now only the purple hair was left.

Juan got on the donkey. Bees and birds flew around his head.

Soon Juan came to a village filled with cats. The cats saw the birds and began to howl. The cats chased the birds.

Then Juan came to a village filled with dogs. The dogs saw the cats and began to growl. The dogs chased the cats.

At last, Juan came to the castle. On the balcony sat the princess. She was very sad.

All at once, she looked up and saw Juan Bobo! Dressed in rags, he carried his sausage. He was followed by a donkey, buzzing bees, flying birds, howling cats, and growling dogs.

Juan held out the sausage and asked, "Would you care for a bite, princess?"

The princess looked at Juan and began to laugh. She laughed and laughed and laughed. She could not stop!

The king was very happy. He asked Juan to live with them at the castle.

So now Juan lives at the castle. He and the princess are very happy.

And where is the purple hair? Juan keeps it under his bed. He has everything he could wish for. He doesn't need it at all!

The Caribbean Islands

Florida

Puerto Rico

Bobo's Magic Wishes is a Puerto Rican folktale. Long ago, Spanish explorers came to Puerto Rico. Today, the major language of Puerto Rico is Spanish. In Spanish, the word *bobo* means "fool." Is Juan Bobo really a fool? Like many folktales, this funny story makes us think about people and human nature.